S0-ARM-178

Sewer Rats

Sewer Rats

Sigmund Brouwer

Orca currents

ORCA BOOK PUBLISHERS

Copyright © 2006 Sigmund Brouwer

All rights reserved. No part of this publication may be reproduced or transmitted in any form or by any means, electronic or mechanical, including photocopying, recording or by any information storage and retrieval system now known or to be invented, without permission in writing from the publisher.

Library and Archives Canada Cataloguing in Publication

Brouwer, Sigmund, 1959-
Sewer rats / Sigmund Brouwer.
(Orca currents)

Issued in print and electronic formats.
ISBN 978-1-55143-527-5 (bound).—ISBN 978-1-55143-488-9 (pbk).—
ISBN 978-1-55143-490-2 (pdf).—ISBN 978-1-55469-712-0 (epub)

I. Title. II. Series.
PS8553.R68467S48 2006   jC813'.54   C2006-900470-6

First published in the United States, 2006
Library of Congress Control Number: 2006921143

Summary: A group known as Sewer Rats take up the challenge of an underground game of paintball.

MIX
Paper from
responsible sources
FSC® C016245

Orca Book Publishers is dedicated to preserving the environment and has printed this book on Forest Stewardship Council® certified paper.

Orca Book Publishers gratefully acknowledges the support for its publishing programs provided by the following agencies: the Government of Canada through the Canada Book Fund and the Canada Council for the Arts, and the Province of British Columbia through the BC Arts Council and the Book Publishing Tax Credit.

Cover photography by Dayle Sutherland
Author photo by Reba Baskett

ORCA BOOK PUBLISHERS
www.orcabook.com

Printed and bound in Canada.

19 18 17 16 • 9 8 7 6

Chapter One

If you ever visit a sewage lagoon, you'll discover what I did. It only takes one good sniff to know it's better to be on the outside, looking in. Sewage lagoons are worse than nasty.

Put it this way. Everything you flush down your toilet goes to the sewage lagoon. That should explain enough.

If you think the contents of one flush is bad, imagine all the toilets in your city filling a pond. If you look close— and you don't want to, trust me—you can even see wads of mushy toilet paper floating in all the brown goop.

Of course, kids aren't supposed to be near the lagoons. There are high steel-link fences to keep people out. On both sides of the lagoon are holding tanks as big as houses. And between those tanks, walkways with guardrails cross over the lagoons.

The new kid, Carter Saylor, was ready to walk above a sewage pond. He wasn't going to use the walkway. His plan was to balance on the guardrail with all the brown goopy stuff right below.

I was happy to be on the outside with my friends, Micky and Lisa. We leaned against the fence, and it bent inward with our weight. I had my fingers wrapped around the linked steel. The sun felt good on my back.

"He's nuts," I said. This was so obvious that Micky and Lisa didn't reply.

Carter pushed off the walkway and onto the rail. He had ragged blond hair almost to his shoulders. He wore black jeans, a black T-shirt and black Nikes.

"Carter must want to be a Sewer Rat real bad," Micky said. "I never thought he would agree to this."

We weren't an official club. But we were known as the Sewer Rats, along with a couple of other kids at school. We fought paintball wars against kids from other schools. But we call them tunnel wars, because we have our paintball fights in the huge pipes of the city storm drain system. Micky takes challenges from kids at other schools who have heard about us and sets up each new war. In the six months since

3

we began, we haven't lost once. It helps that the Sewer Rats know the tunnels better than anyone else.

"He's stupid," Lisa said, staring at Carter. Her voice was angry. "Ugly and stupid."

I half turned my head to look at her.

"Get your eyes off me," Lisa told me. "If I want to think he's stupid, I can. And I can say it too. Unless you want to make something of it."

I've seen Lisa punch guys full in the mouth.

"Nope," I said. "He might be stupid. But I'm not."

Her frown told me it would also be stupid to ask why she hated the new kid so much. All Carter had done was ask us if he could join the Sewer Rats.

Normally we'd let kids try a tunnel war. If a kid wasn't scared to be alone in the darkness below the streets, they could join.

But Lisa had told Carter that all Sewer Rats passed a test at the lagoons. This test: sneaking in and walking the guardrail above the toilet stuff below.

"Stupid or not," Micky said, watching Carter carefully, "you've got to admit he's got guts."

Carter was in plain view on the guardrail. A security guard might notice him any second. His arms were stretched wide as he balanced himself, taking one careful step at a time.

"Guts? I hope he gets caught," Lisa said. "Or falls in."

Her tone made me wonder if there was something I didn't know about Lisa and Carter. Maybe Carter had made the mistake of asking her out. Maybe he wanted to join the Sewer Rats because he wanted to impress her. That would have been dumb. Lisa didn't like guys in that way. Everyone in school knew that. Except for maybe the new kid.

He was now halfway across, walking the guardrail like it was a tightrope.

I thought of the brown toilet stuff in the pond below him. I thought of what might happen if a security guard came by. I started to get a scared feeling in my stomach, a ball of spiders that makes me want to throw up. The same feeling I get every time I go into the tunnels for a paintball war.

Zantor, soldier of the galaxy, I whispered in my head. *Zantor has removed all emotion as he watches the rookie soldier battle the alien swamp.*

By creating this pretend world, I was able to make the ball of spiders stop wriggling in my stomach. I did this when I was scared—in school before a test, and in the tunnels.

Scared as I was in the tunnels, there was no way I could let Micky or Lisa know it. Ever. The Sewer Rats were my only friends. I was more afraid of losing them than I was of the tunnels.

Zantor smiles. The swamp test provides amusement for galaxy soldiers.

The spiders of panic in my stomach stopped wiggling.

Lisa stepped back from the fence. Sounds of nylon and zipper told me that Lisa was opening her backpack. She began to dig through it.

I didn't take my eyes off Carter.

"What's this?" Micky said to Lisa a few second later.

"What's it look like?" she said. "A violin?"

I finally looked over. Lisa had an air horn, the kind that uses pressurized air to make noise. Loud noise.

"Think he'll be able to handle it?" Lisa asked.

"You wouldn't," I said.

"Want to bet?"

"Don't do it," Micky said.

"Don't do what? This?" She pushed the button on the air horn and the sound almost broke my eardrums.

At the walkway, Carter staggered like he had jumped a little at the sudden sound.

Micky spun and shouted at her. "Are you nuts? Don't—"

Lisa cut Micky off by blaring the air horn again.

Lisa blared the air horn in more short blasts.

Two things happened by the lagoon. A big security guard came running around the corner of a holding tank. And Carter saw the security guard and lost his balance. As he fell his head bounced off the guardrail.

Carter dropped into the goop like a giant rock. No splashing around to swim. No coming up for air.

The security guard shouted.

There was still no splashing around, still no sign of Carter.

The security guard dove in after him.

Chapter Two

The next morning we were in Miss Pohl's office. She was our principal.

She looked at us and said one word. "Losers."

That surprised me. Sure, our nickname for her was Bean Pohl because she was tall and slender. She was an older woman. I read somewhere that as people age they get the face they deserve.

Crabby people have a face that looks crabby from all the hours and hours spent with a crabby expression on their face. Mean people get a mask of a face with all their meanness settled right into it.

I think there's truth in that. Miss Pohl has the face of someone who smiles a lot and cares about people. That makes it easy to talk to her. Of all of our teachers, she was the one who seemed most human. And here she was, calling us losers to our faces.

Which is why I was surprised at what she said.

She walked to her window and looked outside for a few seconds.

"Losers," she said again without turning to us.

I was standing at the back wall with Lisa and Micky and Carter. Micky frowned. I touched his elbow. He looked at me. I shook my head. It wouldn't do any good to show that we were mad.

She said it one more time. Sadly. "Losers."

We have all been called much worse before. I know some of the teachers say we're dysfunctional, as if we have a disease.

I've been called a loser before. I'm skinny and dark-haired, with a big nose that's always stuck in a science fiction book. If I'm going to be honest, I'd better admit I'm short too. Okay, really short. But I don't let that bother me. Okay, I do.

Lisa Chambers is blond and pretty in a tough-looking way. She is even tougher than she looks.

Micky Downs? He has a crew cut, square face and big shoulders. He could be one of the best athletes in the school if he ever bothered to try out for a team. As for Carter, I didn't know much about him yet. But if he wanted to be part of our gang, that probably said something about him too.

"It makes me angry," Miss Pohl said, finally facing us again, "when a police officer comes into this school and calls all of you losers. It makes me angry when I hear other people say it too. Because I know it's not true. You are not losers."

She sighed. "I just wish you kids would figure that out before it's too late."

"About the videotape," I began.

"Jim McClosky," she said to me. "Don't give me one of your excuses. It's all there, in black and white."

Who would have thought the city would have video surveillance at a sewage lagoon. Like there's something there to steal.

"It's my fault," Carter said. "They had nothing to do with it. It was my idea. They were just there because they didn't believe I'd be so dumb. I deserve all the punishment."

"Actually," I said. "It's my fault. It was my idea. I deserve the punishment."

"No," Micky said. "It was my idea. I'm the one who should get punished."

Miss Pohl sighed. "Lisa, are you going to try to take the blame too?"

"Not a chance," she said. She fired an angry look at Carter. Another sigh from Miss Pohl.

"I have no choice here," she said. "I've got to take action. I'm told I should suspend the four of you."

She shook her head. "But what good would that do? School is your best chance of proving that you aren't losers. I just wish you kids could see yourselves the way I see you."

"Um," I said, "I'd feel really horrible if you made me miss school for a few days. Please don't suspend us."

"Nice try, McClosky," she said, smiling. "I know you're joking. I also know you have a great imagination. Ever dream of writing stories?"

I'd never considered that. Sure I always ran stories through my head, but to put them on paper?

"And Micky, what do you dream of becoming someday? Lisa? Carter?"

We didn't answer.

"Here's what I'm going to do," she said. "By next Friday, I want a three-page essay from each of you about what you'd like to do most when you're finished school."

"That's it?" Micky said.

"No. There will be some community work involved too. Don't be surprised if it involves scrubbing toilets."

We groaned.

"And please," she said. "Nothing else, all right? If I have to call you in the office again, there will likely be social workers involved."

Not good.

I decided not to mention we had another paintball war in the sewer tunnels the next morning.

Chapter Three

Five Sewer Rats met after school. We stood outside the 7-Eleven. There was Lisa, Micky, the Cooper twins, Al and Dave, and me. The Cooper twins are tall, skinny, redheaded and hardly ever speak.

Their mom and dad are both doctors. You'd think this would be good, but their parents are always either working or on vacation, leaving the Cooper twins with the nanny who has raised them since they were babies.

"It's like this," Micky said to Lisa. "Maybe we should lay low for a while."

"We?" she asked, kicking at a chocolate bar wrapper on the pavement.

"The Sewer Rats. Maybe we should hold off on tomorrow's paintball war against the guys at Medford School. If anything happens and Old Bean Pohl brings in social workers…"

"No way," she said. "Not a chance. We're Sewer Rats. Not sewer chickens."

Her tone didn't scare Micky like it did me.

"Look," he said. "Yesterday—"

"What about it?" she snapped. "Some stupid kid fell in a lagoon and had to be rescued by security. It's not our fault."

I shook my head at the reminder. The guard had pulled Carter from the lagoon. Both of them dripped head to toe with brown, gucky water. Their clothes had slimy lumps all over. The gross part was when the guard had given Carter mouth-to-mouth.

"Not our fault?" Micky said. "Who started with the air horn?"

"Part of the test," she said. "He failed. That's no reason for us to chicken out of the tunnel fight tomorrow."

"But what I'm trying to say," Micky said, "is that everyone in the school— the teachers, Miss Pohl—knows why Carter was in the lagoon."

"That just makes us cool," Lisa said. "Now they know if you want to be a Sewer Rat, you pay the price. Besides, everyone thinks it was funny. I bet even Old Bean Pohl giggled when she saw the video."

Micky started to say something, then shut his mouth as a man in a suit walked past us. The man frowned at us. Once the man was inside the store, Micky said, "Even if they think it's funny, they—"

"The teachers can't do nothing to us," Lisa told him, crossing her arms. The paintball wars aren't on school property.

"But—," Micky tried. It was like trying to stop a hurricane.

"Do you think I care what the teachers think?" Lisa asked. "They think we band together because no one else likes us. And we're proud to agree with them, aren't we?"

Micky shrugged. When people called us losers, it just made our group stronger.

"It's the Medford gang I care about," Lisa continued. "The Sewer Rats have never lost a paintball war and we're not going to chicken out now."

"Hey," the Cooper twins said together. They pointed down the street.

It was Carter on his mountain bike. Headed toward us. The wind blew his blond hair backward.

"What's he doing?" Lisa asked. "Who told him we were going to meet here?"

"I did," Micky said.

"He's not a Sewer Rat!" Lisa was angry.

"After what he went through yesterday, he is," Micky said, crossing his own arms. "You heard him try to take full blame this morning in Old Bean Pohl's office. If he's not in, I'm not in."

Lisa glared at Micky. Micky calmly stared straight into her eyes.

"Come on," I said. "You guys are friends. Think of all the times you've helped each other in the tunnels."

They kept staring at each other.

Carter pulled up, doing a brake slide as he stopped.

"Hey," he said.

The Cooper twins started to sniff the air.

"Very funny," Carter said. "The stuff washes out. Really."

He grinned. "Of course, it took three bottles of shampoo to get clean."

The Cooper twins laughed and gave him high fives.

"What's with those two?" Carter asked me.

Micky and Lisa were still staring at each other.

"Not much," I said. "Any second they're going to kiss and make up."

Finally Lisa uncrossed her arms.

"Are we on for a war with the Medford gang tomorrow?" she asked Micky.

"Sure," he said after a couple of seconds. "With Carter, our new Sewer Rat?"

"Come on, Lisa," Dave Cooper said.

"He passed the test," Al said. "After that, he should be a Sewer Rat."

Lisa darted a dirty look at Carter. "I guess so."

Carter smiled at her.

That was the end of our meeting.

It wasn't until that night as I fell asleep that I began to wonder about Carter.

Because of Lisa's air horn, Carter had fallen into the lagoon. Because of Lisa, Carter was in big trouble. Yet he had ridden up to us as if nothing had happened.

Why wasn't Carter mad at Lisa?

Chapter Four

On Saturday morning, the Sewer Rats met in the tall trees at the edge of Bell Park. Now there were six of us: me and Lisa and Micky, the Cooper twins and Carter.

All of us carried duffel bags that held our helmets and our paintball guns. We knew people would never stop us to ask about our duffel bags because they could have been for soccer or baseball.

On the other hand, plenty of people would have had plenty of questions if we walked around with paintball guns over our shoulders.

And what we were doing, of course, was something we didn't want to be asked about.

Running through the middle of Bell Park was a drainage ditch that led to the river. At the bottom of the big hill that looked down on Bell Park, a big tunnel emptied into this drainage ditch. The tunnel was connected to the entire drainage system below the streets.

It was a big system, a whole maze of tunnels.

The main purpose of the tunnels is to collect water. When it rains, water drains into street gutters. The small streams in the gutters reach grates and drop into the tunnels below the streets.

A one-hour rainstorm might not sound like much, but after a few minutes thousands and thousands of little streams empty into the tunnels.

It adds up. Fast. In fact, after a couple hours of rain, the main tunnel that drains into Bell Park is a solid pipeline of fast-moving water as high as a person's waist.

That's why we never have paintball wars when it looks like it might rain. We don't want to take the chance of getting caught in a flood in the tunnels.

Saturday, though, looked like a great day. The wind was blowing, but there were no clouds. And it didn't matter that the wind was cold. In the tunnels, you only hear the wind when it blows through the grates above.

"Guys," Micky said as we began to walk along a path to take us toward the middle of the park. "Last night, me and Lisa figured on the mousetrap plan. We've heard these Medford guys think they are real commandos. So it only makes sense that we play the waiting game."

He flashed us the big Micky grin. "If they're half as cocky as we've heard, they'll come looking for us. And we can let them walk right into our sights."

"Makes sense," I said. The way it worked in our paintball wars was simple. Each team had a flag. Each team planted it in one spot. The team who reached and took the other team's flag was the winner. "Are we going to use that spot by the underground phone lines?"

"You got it," Micky said. "Sooner or later they have to pass through that area. Me and Lisa mapped out everyone's ambush spot."

Usually, we left the Cooper twins to guard our flag while the rest of us went looking for the other team's flag. With the mousetrap plan, though, we played it different. Even if it took hours without moving, all of us would wait in our hiding spots and gun down the other team's soldiers as they moved in on our flag. Not until most of them had been shot would we go hunting for the other team's flag.

"Remember, it's dark," Micky said. "Don't make any guesses. If you see someone coming and they don't give the password, gun them down."

During our paintball wars, everyone wore helmets with visors for protection from paint bullets. In the dark tunnels, it was hard to tell if a person was an enemy or a friend.

"Today's password?" Al Cooper asked.

"Stinkpot," Micky said.

"Stinkpot?" both twins asked.

Micky grinned. "In honor of Carter's fall into the sewage lagoon."

The twins grinned back. Carter grinned too. Lisa didn't.

Micky tried to get her to grin. "And Lisa, make sure you don't get lost."

We always teased Lisa about the fact that she wasn't good with directions. Actually, I thought Lisa was brave to go into the tunnels even though she might get lost. The only reason I could face going in the tunnels was that I always knew exactly where I was.

Lisa stuck her tongue out at Micky, and that seemed to make things better among us.

We walked in silence for the last five minutes. We reached the drainage ditch. There were trees on both sides. It was dry. We walked along the bottom of the drainage ditch toward the big hill.

We had to step over things that got left behind when the floodwater dropped. There were dolls without heads, old shoes and plastic pop bottles. There was plenty of garbage. All of it had washed from the streets and floated out through the tunnels.

At the tunnel entrance there was a door made of iron bars welded together in squares of about two feet. Dried grass and weeds were wrapped around the bars on the bottom half of the door. They got stuck on the bars as the water flowed through.

The door was attached to the top of the tunnel on large hinges. It was supposed to be locked, but the lock was old and had been loose for as long as we could remember. To get into the tunnel, all you had to do was jiggle the lock until it popped. Then you just lifted the door and slipped inside.

Micky moved to the door. He slapped the lock a few times until it opened. He tested the door by pulling it back. It creaked on rusty hinges.

"Where are they?" Lisa demanded. "You don't think they chickened out, do you?"

Before any of us could answer, there was movement in the bushes above us.

"Chicken? I don't think so," a voice called out.

The Medford School warriors stepped into sight. They had flashlights attached to their belts, their paintball guns ready and their helmets hanging from their hands.

Six of them. Big kids. None of them smiled as they looked down on us.

Chapter Five

It didn't bother me that the Medford warriors were big. Tunnel war was the only place I wasn't scared of big kids. Size worked against them. Skinny, small and fast was much better. And, like I always said, a paintball bullet brought big guys down the same way it brought down anyone else.

"Hey," Micky said. "Come on."

They waited until the guy in front nodded. He had a crew cut and the beginning of a mustache. He looked like the kind of guy who had an army recruiting poster in his bedroom.

Mr. Army marched the rest of the kids toward us. They followed him in single file. When Mr. Army stopped, they stopped. They stayed straight and unmoving with their feet close together and arms at their sides. "At ease, men," he said.

All at the same time, they relaxed and moved their feet shoulder-width apart.

At ease? What kind of freaks were these guys?

Micky stepped over and shook Mr. Army's hand.

Micky always surprised me when he did things like that. Around adults, Micky had attitude. With anyone our age, though, you'd think he was running for student council.

"You know the rules," Micky said.

"Let's go over them again so everyone here knows," Mr. Army said. It sounded like he was clipping his words off with scissors.

"Jim," Micky said to me. "The trophy."

I opened my duffel bag. Beside my paintball gun was our small flag. It was attached to a short wooden pole. I lifted it out and waved it.

"Our flag," Micky said. "If you capture it, it's yours. It will make you kings of the tunnel. No other school has taken our flag since we began the game last year."

Mr. Army spun and pointed to one of his guys. The guy saluted. I mean, actually saluted. Then he reached inside his jacket and took out their team flag.

"Good," Micky said. "We both put our flags somewhere in sight. The war is over when one team takes the other's flag and makes it back here. If we take your flag, we add it to our collection. You can try to get it back next time. But there's a lineup to take us on. Might be a couple months of Saturdays before you get a chance."

"Whatever," Mr. Army said. "I'm not worried. Our guys are tough."

I wondered if they were tunnel tough. It's a different world in there, with the smallest sound echoing in \every direction.

"No paint bullets above the shoulders, right?" Mr. Army asked. It was their army against ours. As we tried to take their flag, we would also be trying to put their soldiers out of the game.

"Right," Micky said. "Someone shoots you high, they're out, you're still in."

We were crazy but we weren't stupid. Paintball bullets hurt badly enough anywhere else on your body. The last place you want to get hit is in the throat.

"Arms and legs are half hits?" Mr. Army asked.

"Yup," Micky told him. "It takes two shots in the arms or legs to put you out. But a shot to the stomach, chest or back is an instant kill. Dead soldiers come out here and wait for the game to end."

"We got it," the Medford guy said. "What else?"

Micky looked at his watch. "You guys are the challengers, so you get to set up first. We give you thirty minutes to hide your flag before we go into the tunnels. Then you wait where you are and give us thirty minutes. If you head in now, the war will start at eleven o'clock. After that, anyone moving in the tunnels is fair game."

"Any boundaries in there? In Cadets, they limit the size of the field for war games. Otherwise we could be down there for hours."

"You'll find out soon enough that the boundaries are set by the size of the tunnels. Most of the sewers are too small to move through."

"Got it," Mr. Army said. It looked like he wanted to salute.

"Good luck," Micky said.

Mr. Army rubbed at his mustache. "We don't need luck."

"If you say so," Micky said. He pointed at the sky. "One other thing. It's clear now, but you never know in an hour or two. If it starts to rain and you see any water in the tunnels, the game is off. No matter if one team is up by five warriors. Everyone leaves the tunnel and we come back to fight another day. Got it?"

"Got it." Mr. Army turned and faced his gang.

"Men, prepare for battle," he barked.

They all put their helmets on at the same time. They looked like robots.

"About face," Mr. Army barked.

They all turned toward the black hole of the tunnel. They didn't move toward it though.

"Move out, men," Mr. Army said.

The Medford guys began to march. The guy who reached the tunnel first held the door open so the others could slip inside. One by one, they stepped into the darkness of the tunnel. Each one of them had to crouch to move inside.

When they were all inside, Mr. Army barked out again. This time his voice had a weird echo from the concrete walls of the tunnel.

"Let the operation begin," he said.

All together, they began to march forward. The echo of their footsteps continued to reach us long after they had disappeared into the darkness.

And then there was silence, broken only by the whistling of the wind in the trees.

Chapter Six

We waited ten minutes to open our duffel bags and take out our paintball guns. There was no sense in having all the stuff out in the open, just in case somebody wandered along and decided to ask questions.

We loaded our paintballs. Think of gum balls filled with paint. That's what a paintball bullet is. An expensive paintball gun is accurate up to one hundred feet away.

Does it hurt when a paintball hits you? It's about the same as getting hit by a tennis ball—a really fast tennis ball. That's why we wore layers of clothing for protection: sweatshirts with jean jackets over top. We also made sure our necks were covered with scarves. Get hit there, and you'd have a bruise for weeks.

All of us had pump-action guns. The semi-automatics fired paintballs faster, but none of us could afford the more expensive guns or all the ammo they wasted. Not even the Cooper twins, because, rich as their parents were, they hated giving money to their sons.

Once the paintball guns were loaded, we took our helmets from our backpacks. We put the helmets in place, visors up. We checked our flashlights. Then we were ready. We counted down the final seconds.

Exactly thirty minutes after the Medford gang had gone into the tunnels, we followed. Micky held the gate open for us to go inside. He let it fall behind him. We all stepped forward into the darkness.

Twenty steps into the tunnel, we stopped. We waited for our eyes to adjust to the dark. We had not put the visors down on our helmets yet. There was no need. We had a half hour of our own to get ready for battle.

As we waited, I took a deep breath. Like always, the approaching panic felt like a ball of spiders in my stomach. I reminded myself who I was.

Zantor, soldier of the galaxy. His nerves are steel-cold bands as he plunges deep into the alien nest. Upon him depends the freedom of the entire galaxy. Zantor will defeat the enemy. Zantor has never failed. Women of great beauty wait to adore him upon his return. Women of great, great beauty. Women who will—

"Jim," Micky whispered. "Take us there, buddy."

"Sure," I said. I told myself I would get back to Zantor and his beautiful women as soon as I had a chance.

I moved to the front of our short line and began to lead. They followed. All of us wore Nike's with soft soles. I was the only one who didn't have to duck as we walked through the cool darkness of the tunnel. That was one thing that really helped me in the tunnels.

The other thing was my mind map. I knew exactly where to go.

For some reason, I am good at making maps in my head. All I do is pretend I'm a bird looking down. I keep track of turns and twists, and I never get lost in the tunnels.

Not that getting lost for long is something anyone would have to worry about. For one thing, it's not totally dark. Every forty or fifty steps, there are grates above. Or, in some tunnels, manhole covers. These openings not only let in water, but light.

Also, there is a difference in size between the main tunnel and all the others. The main tunnel is big enough to walk through nearly standing. The tunnels that feed into the main tunnel are a foot and a half smaller. You have to crouch to get through them. These connect to even smaller tunnels that you need to crawl through.

So if you ever want to get out, you just follow a small tunnel to a bigger tunnel, and a bigger tunnel to the main tunnel.

How do you know which direction to go?

Easy. Drop a marble.

All of the tunnels slope toward the main tunnel. If they didn't, the water would never drain out. Watch which way the marble rolls, and you'll know which way to go.

Of course we didn't want out. We wanted to reach the central part of the tunnels. Which is why my mental map was so helpful. I knew exactly how to get us there.

I turned my flashlight on and hung it from the back of my pants. The sunlight from the grates was enough to allow me to see where I was going, so I didn't need the flashlight myself. By hanging it behind me, I made it easier for everyone else to follow me.

At each grate in the gutters above, we passed through beams of sunlight. It was colder in the tunnel than it had been outside. Mist seemed to hang in those sunlight beams. Our breath made a weird soft sound as it bounced off the concrete walls. The tunnel smelled like a mixture of dirty socks and rotting tomatoes.

Even with my mental map, I didn't like it much here. Above were buses and cars. The concrete of the tunnels was old and cracked in places. It had rained a lot over the last month. I wondered if the dirt was heavy with water and ready to cave through the old concrete.

Then my mind really started working. I told myself it could rain hard and fast and trap us with floodwater. Rats could swarm us. Or maybe pythons had escaped from pet stores and found a place down here. And a guy always heard about alligators loose in the sewer tunnels below New York and—

STOP! I told myself.

This was Zantor, galaxy soldier, leading his troops. He feared nothing.

I turned my mind back to getting us to our mousetrap spot. It was far ahead in the semi-darkness, where three tunnels joined the main tunnel, like spokes at the center of a wheel.

In the center of the main tunnel, a manhole cover gave good light. That's where we would plant the flag. It would be easy to see and would draw the Medford guys like mice to cheese.

And we would be hiding in the side tunnels, ready to gun them down.

That, at least, was the plan.

Chapter Seven

Ten minutes later, we arrived at the place we called the mousetrap. Above was the manhole cover. The light coming through the circles in the cover made ghostly white plates on the tunnel floor. The rumble of cars overhead was hardly louder than the sound of someone clearing their throat.

For a few seconds, none of us spoke. Something about the tunnels always made a person quiet.

"All right," Micky finally whispered. "Jim, buddy, you plant the flag."

There was a ladder leading down from the manhole. I climbed halfway up the ladder. With an old shoelace, I tied the flagpole to a ladder rung. The shaft of light fell on the edge of the flag.

I climbed back down.

"Good," Micky said. "Now we guard it. Lisa, you get everyone in the positions we went through last night."

"You both packed blankets, right?" she asked the Cooper twins. "After Micky called you last night."

"Right," Al said. "He said we'd be on the ground."

"Exactly." Lisa pointed down at the first small tunnel. "Both of you take that tunnel. Follow it until you come to the cross tunnel. When you get there, lie on the ground feet to feet, with one of you facing each direction. Your blankets should help you. And remember, no noise."

They left, ducking to move through the smaller tunnel.

"Carter..." She spit on the ground. She could have been clearing her throat. But I didn't think so. Not by the tone of her voice. "You take the far tunnel. If you go about fifteen steps up the tunnel, you'll find a big breaker box. You can hide behind it."

Not only were these tunnels used to drain water, they held a lot of underground pipes and wiring.

"Sure," he said in a cheerful voice. It sounded like he was going to do his best to remain sweet, no matter how Lisa treated him. "A breaker box?"

"For telephone wires," Micky said. "There's no danger from electricity."

"Cool," Carter said.

Lisa spit on the ground again. "Take your spot. Wait and don't move until me or Micky calls you out. Don't even scratch your nose. Your best chance is if they don't know you're there."

"Gotcha," Carter said. "Whatever it takes."

He disappeared into the darkness of the far tunnel.

"Micky's got the third small tunnel," Lisa told me. "And I'm going back up the main tunnel. They might try to sneak in behind us."

"I take my usual spot?" I asked.

"Yup," she said. "You're our ace in the hole. If they get past any of us, we need you to be good. Real good."

No fears, I thought. *Zantor is the best.*

Micky and Lisa split and went in opposite directions. In a few seconds they were just dark shadows. Then nothing.

I went to the side of the main tunnel. Large plastic pipes ran along the side of the tunnel. I guessed they held cables for television. The plastic protected them from water damage.

More important, the pipes were great protection for me. I could slide underneath them and be totally hidden from anyone who came to take the flag.

If any of the Medford school warriors managed to get this far, I would wait until they were halfway up the ladder. Then I would roll out from under the pipes and come out, firing paintball bullets.

I set my paintball rifle down and pulled a blanket out of my backpack. It would make my wait on the concrete easier. I knelt down and smoothed the blanket on the rough floor of the tunnel.

I crawled on it. I hoped no bugs wanted to drop from the pipes above into my ear.

I checked my glow-in-the-dark watch. Five minutes until the battle started.

I thought of the Medford warriors. Somewhere in the tunnels they were getting ready to hunt us down. Would they spread out or come at us in a wave?

The spiders of panic began to wriggle again in my stomach.

Zantor lives for moments like this. Moments that would strain a lesser man's heart to the point of failure. Zantor does not fear. No. The most awesome warrior in the galaxy feeds on the fear of others.

The spiders of panic went away.

I was grateful that sunlight squeezed through the small holes of the manhole cover. Without those pale circles of light, it would have been completely dark.

I can't stand complete darkness. Once, when I was little, I accidentally locked myself in a dark room. No one found me for hours. All I remember is screaming and imagining bugs crawling over my leg. And...*Zantor has no bad memories*, I told myself. *Zantor is a rock. He feels nothing.*

That got my mind back to the paintball war.

Zantor strains his razor sharp hearing for the sound of approaching aliens. Zantor waits with patience. Zantor is the greatest hunter of them all.

I waited. And waited some more.

When the sound did arrive, it took a moment for me to understand what I was hearing.

Blam! Blam! Blam!

It was the thud of paintball bullets. Followed by a loud scream of pain.

And as the scream died, I heard the pounding of feet running down the tunnel—away from me.

Chapter Eight

At first, I did nothing. Not because I was afraid. It surprised me, but I was too busy trying to figure out what was happening.

Beyond me, in the darkness, I heard moaning.

"Oh man," a voice croaked. "This hurts. I can hardly breathe. Help me. Somebody help me."

Still I did nothing. Maybe the Medford warriors were trying to fake us out. A month earlier, we had done the same thing to another team. Lisa pretended to be hurt. When the other team came out of hiding, we splattered them with paintballs.

"Micky?" the voice croaked. "Lisa? Jimmy? Help me…"

Using names didn't mean anything. The Medford guys knew all of us by name. Anyone in paintball did. The Sewer Rats were legends among all the warriors. It would be easy for them to call out our names to fool us.

"Come on. I can't see. Jimmy, help me. Lisa…Micky…"

The voice died again, like whoever was calling could hardly get enough air into his lungs.

Zantor, soldier of the galaxy, was hidden in the battlefield. He heard his name. Was it an alien trick? Or did someone truly need him? Zantor must think quickly.

All right, I thought. The Cooper twins were farther away, so it couldn't be one of them. If it was, one would be helping the other. Or I would be hearing two voices.

Not them then. If it was Micky, he wouldn't have called out his own name. Same with Lisa. So if it was any of us, it had to be Carter.

"Blind...help...hurry..."

Sounds fool you in the tunnel. You never know where they're coming from. It could be Carter at the breaker box or one of the Medford warriors somewhere else.

Were the aliens trying to lure Zantor into the open?

"Please...please..."

If they were acting, this person was doing a great job.

What would Zantor do?

I decided to take a risk. If it was a trick, the Medford warriors wouldn't find me just from my voice. I was too well hidden beneath the pipes. The tricky echoes would also fool them.

"Carter?" I called out. "Is that you?"

"Hurry man! It hurts!"

"What's the password?" I said, raising my voice.

"Stink...pot..."

This was no trick!

I rolled out from under the pipe. I got to my feet and snapped on the flashlight as I began to run to Carter's hiding spot.

Within seconds, I reached him. He had fallen beside the breaker box. Clumps of dirt were on the ground beside him. There was dirt on his shoulders. But it wasn't the dirt that got my attention.

My flashlight beam showed fresh red paint splattered all over the wall behind him.

I lowered the light to his face. And saw exactly why he was in so much pain.

He'd taken the paintball bullets in the head. It shouldn't have hurt him, but the visor of his helmet had been open.

Red paint covered his face like blood. I was worried some of it might not be paint.

"Hang in there," I told him. "We'll get you out right away."

He nodded and gulped. Then his eyes closed.

"Micky, Micky!" I shouted down the tunnels. "Micky!"

Chapter Nine

I hate hospitals. I think it's from when my dad died. I can't remember much because I was only four. But I remember the smells and the big hallways and people in white walking in all directions and ignoring me. Most of all, I remember how afraid I was because everyone around me seemed so afraid.

That Sunday afternoon it all came back to me as Micky and I looked for Carter's room in the hospital. I was already nervous because of what happened to Carter. I wanted to throw up.

Micky must have been nervous too. He didn't say much. Not until we got to room 1875.

"We should have brought him comic books or something," Micky said.

"Except what if he can't read?" I asked. That was my big fear. That Carter was blind. He'd taken paintball bullets in the face. Not good.

The day before, while the Cooper twins and Micky helped Carter out of the tunnel, I had run ahead to call an ambulance. Then I had called his folks, who went straight to the hospital to meet him. Our last view of Carter had been of the medics loading him into the ambulance. This morning we had no idea what to expect.

Micky knocked on the door.

"Come in," a man's voice said.

We pushed through the door.

Carter was in bed, wearing green hospital pajamas. He had a white eye patch taped over his left eye. His face was the color of chopped meat.

I gulped.

A man stood up beside Carter's bed. He was big, with dark hair, a wide face and a thick mustache. There was a mole on his left cheek. He wore blue jeans and a sweatshirt.

"I'm Carter's father," he said. "John Saylor."

For some reason, I felt like I had seen him before.

"Micky," Micky said to him. Micky didn't go over and shake the man's hand. Micky doesn't like anyone who has any authority. This includes all adults.

"Jim," I said, standing a little ways behind Micky. The man didn't seem to recognize me, so I decided I was wrong about seeing him before.

"Hey, guys," Carter said. His voice sounded much better. "Dad, these two helped me get out of the tunnel."

I winced. We had enough trouble coming down on us from all the adults in our lives. It looked like we'd never have another paintball fight again. Now I figured Carter's father would want to tell us how stupid we were.

Instead of frowning and ripping into us, Carter's father smiled.

"I want to thank you guys for your quick thinking in there. You made all the right moves."

Micky found his voice. "You're not mad at us?"

"At first I was," Mr. Saylor said. "I've heard some of the sewer tunnels are old enough to collapse, and I didn't like knowing that you guys were in there."

"That will change," Micky said. "Everybody has made us promise not to go in there again. And we'll stick to our promise."

"Good," Mr. Saylor said. "And from what Carter explained, you guys made sure everyone in these paintball wars followed safety rules. It was just a bad break that he hadn't closed his visor."

"A real bad break," Carter said. "I think my watch was a little slow. I didn't think it was going to get started for a few minutes. I had my visor half open so I could breathe better. I was sitting against the wall, and *boom*, out of nowhere two guys appear and start firing. It was like they knew exactly where I was."

He touched his face. "Good thing the bullets caught the edge of my visor and slowed some of the impact. Otherwise I might have lost an eye."

I pointed at his eye patch. "You can see?"

"Doctors say everything will be fine in a few days," Carter told me.

"Again, thanks to you guys getting him out so fast," said Mr. Saylor. He smiled at Micky. "Of course, that shouldn't be a surprise. I know your father was a hero."

An angry look crossed Micky's face. He opened his mouth to say something. Then he changed his mind and closed it. He turned around and left the room without saying a word.

"Did I say something wrong?" Mr. Saylor asked.

"Yeah, but it's not your fault," I said.

Once, and only once, Micky had spoken to me about his dad: a cop at a car accident. He went into a burning car to rescue a woman. The car had exploded. Micky thought heroes were useless.

He'd rather have a father than someone everyone called a hero. Micky got mad at anyone who told him he should be proud that his father had given up his life trying to help someone.

"What is it?" Carter's dad asked me. "What made him mad?"

"Not a big deal," I said.

It was, of course. But it was Micky's business, not mine.

"Well," I said, "got to go. Get better, Carter."

That was the end of the hospital visit.

I found Micky in the hallway. He was pacing back and forth.

I didn't say anything. Micky burns slow. I didn't figure talking would do any good.

"I've been thinking," Micky said when he looked up at me. "We got to go."

"Sure," I said. If he wanted to pretend nothing had happened, that was fine. "Where?"

"Let me ask you something. Did you hear what Carter told us? About when he got hit?"

"I was right there with you," I said. "I'm small, but I'm not deaf."

"Well?" Micky asked.

"Well what?" I asked back.

"Carter said it was like they knew exactly where he was."

"And?" I said.

"If Carter's watch was slow, they probably fired as soon as they knew it was time to start the paintball war. You know, right on the hour. Like they did know exactly where he was. Like they were waiting to gun him down as soon as they could."

It hit me. If that was true, there was only one way they could have known.

"You don't think…"

"Yes, I do." He smiled grimly. "Which is why we are leaving this hospital right now."

Chapter Ten

Yesterday's wind had become colder. Low dark clouds hung heavy. There was nothing to enjoy about our bike ride to Lisa's house. Not the weather. Not what Micky and I knew we had to ask her.

Lisa's mother answered the door of their small house.

"Good afternoon," she said. Mrs. Chambers pushed some hair from her face. She was blond like Lisa, but her face was tired. "You two aren't here for paintball or anything, are you?"

"No, ma'am," Micky said.

"Good," Mrs. Chambers said. "I have a hard time keeping her out of trouble."

"Is Lisa home?" Micky asked. "We just want to talk to her."

"In her bedroom, I think," Mrs. Chambers said. "I'll go get her. Meet me in the kitchen. I'll see if I can find you something to eat."

She gave us a smile, a tired one, but still a smile. "Don't think I'm upset with you about yesterday. You two are good guys. And I understand kids trying to have fun. I'm just glad you promised not to go into the sewer tunnels from now on."

We nodded as we stepped past her into the house.

"How's that boy who was hurt?" she asked.

"He's all right," Micky said. "He's got an eye patch, but the doctors say it will be off soon."

She smiled a grown-up smile. "That's good. I'll get Lisa."

Micky and I waited in the kitchen as Mrs. Chambers went to get Lisa. We sat at the table. Lisa got there a few seconds later, with Mrs. Chambers behind her.

"What?" Lisa said.

Not hello or how are you. But that was Lisa.

"We need to talk," Micky said.

"No, we don't," Lisa said.

"Yes, we do," Micky said.

Mrs. Chambers coughed.

"Mom," Lisa said, "it's okay. People don't have to talk nice to each other all the time. That's pretending. You know I don't like pretending."

"Do you want me to stay?" Mrs. Chambers asked her.

"It's fine with me," Lisa said. "I have nothing to hide."

"What about the way that you set Carter up to get blasted in the tunnel?" Micky said. "Think we wouldn't figure it out?"

"Go away," she told us.

I had hoped Lisa would frown the way she frowned in class when she couldn't figure out an answer. I had hoped she wouldn't know what Micky was talking about.

But this sounded like she knew exactly what Micky meant.

"Why do you hate him so much?" Micky asked. "He's a good guy."

"Go away," Lisa said.

"No," Micky said, "not until I have an answer."

"How's this?" Lisa pushed Micky in the chest.

Then she turned and ran out of the kitchen. A few seconds later, we heard the front door slam.

"Lisa!" Mrs. Chambers said. "Lisa!"

She ran after her daughter.

"Wow," I said, "that wasn't exactly what I expected."

"No," Micky said, "but I'd say it proves she set up Carter, doesn't it?"

"But why?" I asked. "He just moved to town. Why would she hate him so much?"

A half-second later I stood up. I pointed at the fridge behind Micky's shoulder.

"I think," I said, "I may have the answer."

Chapter Eleven

"What?" Micky said. "Food?"

"Not in the fridge. On top." There was a framed photo that had caught my eye. "The photo. Look."

Micky stood and moved closer. He whistled. "I don't get it. That's Carter's dad."

Micky and I had been in this kitchen more than a couple of times before.

Now I understood why I knew I'd seen Mr. Saylor before. It was this photo. He was standing on a dock at a lake, holding a big fish in one hand and a fishing rod in the other. He had the same mustache and mole on his cheek. Beside him, Mrs. Chambers and Lisa both squinted into the sun. It was an old photo. Lisa was much smaller.

"Carter's dad," Micky repeated. "I don't get it."

Before I could say anything, Mrs. Chambers returned to the kitchen.

"Lisa's gone," Mrs. Chambers said. "She yelled that she was going to Bell Park and that she wanted to be left alone. She's been in a bad mood for a while."

"We understand," Micky said. Micky paused. He pointed at the fridge. "By the way, who is the man in that photo?"

"Oh," Mrs. Chambers said. "That's Lisa's father."

She stopped for a second. When she spoke again, her voice was quiet. "We haven't been married for some time. He left town years ago and just moved back."

"Lisa's father," Micky said. "But the kid in the—"

It was my turn to elbow Micky.

"Let's go before it rains," I said to Micky.

"Sure, but—"

I grabbed his arm and pulled him away before he could tell Mrs. Chambers anything about Carter and the man in the hospital.

This was something Lisa should explain. But if my guess was right, there wasn't much left to explain.

We didn't find Lisa in Bell Park. Instead, we found her bicycle. At the edge of the drainage ditch at the far end of the park—near the sewer tunnel entrance.

"Is she inside?" I asked.

Micky looked at the dark sky. He held his hand out, feeling for drops of rain.

"I hope not," Micky said. "It's going to rain any second. And rain hard. You know what that means."

I nodded. It meant a lot of water. The drainage ditch was empty now, but during a hard rainstorm, it would fill with fast, muddy water higher than my waist—like a flash flood.

I moved to the iron bars at the front of the tunnel and looked inside. It was just a black hole—a huge black hole. If she had decided to hide in the sewer tunnels, it could be years before we found her. And that was only if she didn't hide.

I thought about the rain. If she was in there, Micky and I needed to warn her.

But if she wasn't in the tunnels, we would be putting ourselves in danger for nothing.

"Lisa?" I yelled. "Lisa?"

"Don't yell," she said in a grumpy voice. "It hurts my ears."

I nearly had a heart attack. I never expected her to be so close. As my eyes adjusted to the darkness, I saw her outline. She was sitting inside the tunnel, about twenty steps away.

"Come on out," Micky said, moving beside me. "We want to talk."

"No," she said.

"What do you mean *no*?" Micky asked.

"It's a two-letter word for buzz off."

From where Lisa sat, Micky and I would be two dark figures against the light of the sky.

"We want to talk," Micky said.

"Buzz off," she said.

"But—"

"Buzz off," she repeated. "Or don't you understand English? Maybe I should tell you in French."

I smiled a little. Her bicycle spoke more French than she did.

"I came here to be alone," she said. "I wanted to go where nobody would bug me. So in case you haven't figured it out, I don't want to talk."

"You have to talk," Micky said.

"Why?" came her voice.

"Because we know about you and Carter."

Silence from inside the tunnel.

"We saw his dad in the hospital today," Micky told her. "It's the same guy in the photo at your house."

Silence—but only for a second. I saw her outline as she got to her feet and turned away from us. As my eyes understood what was happening, my ears heard the pounding of her feet as she ran deeper into the tunnel.

"Lisa!" Micky shouted. "Lisa! Stop!"

She didn't. The echo of her footsteps faded. Then there was nothing but the blackness of the tunnel—with Lisa somewhere inside.

"Nuts," Micky said. He kicked at a rock. "Dumb girl."

Before I could say anything, a crack of lightning caught the corner of my eye. A crash of thunder rolled over us.

And it began to pour.

Chapter Twelve

"Now what?" I yelled above the rain. Heavy hard drops pounded my skull. Within seconds, my hair was soaked like I had just taken a shower.

Micky didn't answer. He grabbed my arm and pulled me toward the tunnel. He popped open the cage door and pulled me inside.

"At least in here we'll be dry," he said.

Not for long, I thought.

I looked outside. The sky had disappeared. All I saw were gray sheets of water. Already there were puddles in the drainage ditch. Soon the puddles would join and begin to flow. Soon water would be flowing beneath our feet from this tunnel.

"We've got to get her out of here," I said. "If it doesn't stop raining…"

"She's got a brain and two feet," he said. "She can get herself out."

"Come on, Micky. Of all of us, she's the one who gets lost the easiest. Remember the day we had to go looking?"

I was telling the truth. We both knew it. Lisa had a terrible sense of direction. After one paintball war, it had taken her two hours to find her way out. Since then, she has stayed with one of us during the paintball battles.

"Look," Micky snapped. "I'm no hero."

"Oh." I knew better than to say anything else.

We waited five minutes in silence— at least silence from talk. All the noise came from the rain. It was like an army of drummers.

A small stream of water began to trickle at our feet. Not from our wet hair and wet clothes. But from the streets and gutters that fed these tunnels.

I started walking up the tunnel.

"What are you doing?" he asked.

I turned.

"Micky, I'm no hero either. But Lisa knows as much as we do how important it is to clear out when the water starts to run. If she hasn't made it here by now, it's because she can't."

"How are you going to find her?" he asked. "There are dozens of smaller tunnels she could have taken."

"I don't know," I said. "But I've got to try."

I knew if something happened to her and I hadn't done my best to help, I would feel guilty for the rest of my life.

"Even if it kills you?" Micky said. "Heroes are stupid. Dead heroes are even stupider."

"Getting killed is not part of my plan," I said.

I began to walk farther into the tunnel. The stream of water was now deeper. Already it had started to push over top of the toes of my shoes.

I repeated my words to myself.

Getting killed was not part of the plan.

Chapter Thirteen

I should have known I'd become afraid.
I had been so worried about Lisa and
the water that I forgot what happens
when the darkness closes around me.

Now, in complete darkness, I felt so
lonely that my chest hurt. When I was
a kid and had to be in the dark, I used
to believe that people and sunlight and
laughter did not exist. I felt the same now.

Except there was one thing that made me feel different: the sound of the water—water that grew faster and stronger as all the streets above poured water into these tunnels.

As the spiders of panic wriggled, I turned myself into…

Zantor!

The soldier of the galaxy will never die. He bats away danger as if it were a pesky fly. His legs are so strong, no river can sweep him away. And he will save the beautiful woman. She will wrap her arms around him and pull her face close. She will—

"Jim!" Micky shouted from behind me. "Hang on!"

Someday I would have to tell Micky not to get in the way of Zantor and his beautiful women. But this was not the day.

Zantor was glad to have help.

"Micky," I said as he caught up to me. "Thanks, man."

"Don't thank me for being stupid. Maybe it's my fault she ran away. You know, because I talked about Carter and her dad."

"It's not your fault," I said. "She can't run away from that stuff forever."

Micky put his hand on my shoulder and squeezed. It made me feel a lot taller.

"So," he said. "Where did she go?"

"My guess is she stayed in the main tunnel as far as possible. If she was trying to get away from us, it's easier to run in this tunnel than in the smaller ones. Besides, she's probably afraid of getting lost in one of the side tunnels."

We passed beneath a tiny waterfall from the street grate above. We stepped through the gray light from the grate. It showed the water at our feet collecting into a small stream.

"What if she took a side tunnel?"

"If she is trying to get away from us, she wouldn't have gone in too far. She should be able to hear us."

Ahead, the wall of the tunnel was a little darker, showing where a smaller tunnel ran into this one.

I stopped. "Lisa!" I yelled into the side tunnel. "Are you there?"

We waited a couple of seconds. No answer.

We moved on. By now, the stream had risen to our ankles. Water splashed halfway up my shins.

"Lisa!" Micky yelled at the next tunnel. "Lisa!"

That's how it went for the next few minutes. We stopped and yelled into every tunnel that branched into the main tunnel. I was so scared for her that even Zantor, soldier of the galaxy, was getting afraid.

We reached the mousetrap place where the three other tunnels joined the main tunnel. Water poured through the holes in the manhole cover above. The place where I had been lying beneath plastic pipes was completely covered with water. The stream was halfway to our knees and sucked at our legs with every step we took.

"Think about it," I said. "We waited about five minutes before going after her. Running at full speed, she could get this far, but not much farther."

"And?"

"It took about five minutes for the water to start. She wouldn't have been much farther than this before she noticed. She would have turned around, right?"

"Right," he said. He had to raise his voice. The sounds of the rushing water forced both of us to yell. "So why haven't we seen her yet?"

I grabbed his arm.

"Listen!" I shouted.

I pointed in the direction I thought I might have heard noise.

He turned his head that way, leaning in to listen better.

For a few seconds, we heard only the rush of water.

Then...

"Help! Help!"

It was a faint sound. But there was no mistake. Ahead, from the tunnel to our right, came Lisa's voice.

We almost tripped over each other in our hurry to get there.

We left the faint light from the manhole cover and moved into the darkness ahead.

"Help!" It was clearer now. "Help!"

I was in front. So I hit it first. A solid wall where there should have been tunnel.

Micky ran into me.

"Hey!" he said. "Why'd you stop?"

"No choice," I shouted at him. "Part of the tunnel wall must have fallen."

I tried to picture it as if I had a flashlight. The dirt above was heavy with all the water from the spring rains of the last month. The concrete of the tunnels was old. I remembered that I had seen dirt near here, beside Carter. The concrete must have been cracking then. Now it had finally fallen.

"A cave-in," I said to Micky.

He pushed past me. He reached around with his hands. A few seconds later, he spoke to me.

"There's an opening at the top."

"And she's on the other side, right?"

He didn't answer me.

"Lisa!" he shouted. "Can you hear me?"

"Yes, yes, yes!"

"Are you all right?" he shouted.

"My foot is stuck," she said.

"We'll run and get help."

"No!" Even in the confusion of the water and the darkness, the fear in her voice reached us.

"No?"

"The water," she cried. "It's already at my knees!"

That's when I noticed. The floor on our side was dry. There was no stream running over our feet. No stream adding to the big one in the main tunnel.

And there was only one reason.

This fallen part had made more than a wall. It had made a dam. All the water on the other side was rising. And Lisa was trapped there with a stuck foot.

Chapter Fourteen

Zantor thought quickly. Seconds later, Zantor knew what to do.

"Micky," I said. "The opening at the top. Can you tell how big it is?"

I waited a few seconds as he felt around in the dark.

"Big enough to get through," he said, guessing why I had asked.

"Then one of us needs to help Lisa on the other side," I said. "And one of us needs to go back to the main tunnel to go for help. The ladder there reaches the manhole cover. It's the fastest way out."

A clump of dirt fell from the tunnel roof and hit my shoulder. Was another big piece going to cave in?

"Good plan," he said. "But who goes for help?"

Spiders of panic grew big in my stomach again. Whoever stayed behind would have to crawl through the small opening. I thought of the tunnel roof pressing down on me. I wanted to run.

"Who goes for help?" Micky asked again. "I mean, it's not fair to the person who has to stay behind."

"We'll do it this way," I said. "I'm going to put my hand behind my back. I'll hold up one finger. Or two. If you call it right, you go for help. Call it wrong, I go."

"But—"

"Can you think of a better way?"

"No," he said.

I put my hand behind my back. I made a fist and held out one finger.

Micky waited.

"Come on," I said. "Guess. We don't have much time."

"Two," Micky said. "Two fingers."

He had guessed wrong. All I had to do was show him my hand—with one finger showing—and I was free.

I brought my hand up with two fingers sticking out.

"Can you see it in this darkness?" I asked.

He reached for my hand and felt both fingers.

"Two," he said.

A trickle of water ran onto the floor of the tunnel. Somewhere, this wall had sprung a leak. Water from the other side was getting through.

"You called it right," I told Micky. "You go for help."

"Are you sure?" he asked.

"Very sure," I said. "That's what we agreed."

Micky was too big. I had a better chance of getting through to Lisa. Plus he was strong enough to push away the manhole cover to get to the street above. As much as I wanted to go, it didn't make sense for him to stay behind. I knew I would never like myself if I ran away now.

"Lisa!" I shouted before I could change my mind. "Hang on! I'm coming in!"

I put my hand on Micky's shoulder. "Give me a hand. Get me up to the opening. Then go for help as fast as you can."

Micky boosted me high enough for my head and shoulders to reach the hole. I pulled forward. He pushed my feet.

And then I was totally into the opening above the wall.

I began to pull my way over the rough dirt and pieces of concrete.

Chapter Fifteen

I was breathing fast. It seemed like I couldn't get air into my lungs. I wanted to scream.

Lisa beat me to the scream.

"Hurry," she cried from the other side. "The water is nearly at my waist!"

It was like a slap across my face.

I pulled myself forward. My fingers dug into dirt. My belly scraped over pieces of concrete. I wondered if I would get stuck. The fear hit me. I needed...

Zantor, soldier of the galaxy. He moves ahead. He is fearless. The odds are against him. Yet because he is so powerful he will—

Stop, I told myself.

I was crawling over the top of a cave-in. The roof might fall on me any second. On the other side, rising water might drown me. And Lisa. It wasn't wrong to be afraid.

In fact, only an idiot wouldn't be afraid.

I didn't need Zantor. I needed me. I needed to get to Lisa and help her. And I needed to lose my fear of being afraid. I needed to keep moving forward.

I pulled myself ahead, keeping my head down, hoping my shoulders wouldn't get stuck.

Then, without warning, my fingers clawed at air.

"Lisa?"

"Here!"

She was so close I could almost…

I did. My hands reached her hands.

"Lisa, Lisa!"

I kicked ahead and began to fall. She kept hold of my hands. I splashed into the water beside her.

It was totally dark.

"Jimmy!" She grabbed my wrist. "Jimmy!"

"Micky's gone for help," I said. "I'm going to stay with you."

"He's got to hurry," she said. "The water. I can't believe how fast it's rising."

The water was cold. Very cold. Above my waist.

"You told us you can't move," I said. "What happened?"

"My foot is under a piece of concrete," she said. "I was just turning to go back when the roof fell in. I tried to jump back but I didn't get far enough."

"Wait," I said. "I'm going to go under."

I sucked in a deep breath and closed my eyes. I ducked beneath the water as it bubbled around my head. I reached around until my hand bumped into Lisa's knee. I followed her leg downward until my hand got to her ankle.

I felt the chunk of concrete that had trapped her foot.

I brought my other hand around and got hold of the concrete block with both hands.

I tugged.

Nothing happened.

I tugged again.

Still nothing.

I was running out of air.

I tried one last time.

It didn't move at all. The rest of my body was in the water, and when I pulled, all I did was pull myself closer to the rock.

No air left.

I stood. When I broke free of the water, I gasped.

"I can't move it," I said.

She wrapped her arms around me. "I'm so afraid," she said.

"Me too."

We stayed that way for a few seconds. Then she let go of me.

"This is my fault," she said. "All because I hated Carter. I didn't mean for him to get hurt. I just wanted him out of the paintball game. I wanted him to look stupid for getting caught right away."

"You told the warriors where he would be, didn't you?" I said. "It had to be you. Only you and Micky knew where Carter would be waiting."

"I didn't want him to be part of our gang," she said.

"Because of your dad, right?" I asked. "He's now Carter's stepdad."

"When Dad and Mom split up a few years ago, Dad moved out of town,"

Lisa said. "When Dad married again, his new wife already had two kids. Carter was one of them. And they just moved back to town. It isn't fair that Carter gets my dad when I want so much for him to be with Mom and me."

She started to cry. I never thought someone as tough as Lisa would cry. It gave me an idea of how much she had been holding inside.

"Why did Carter want to join the Sewer Rats?" I asked. "I mean, he must have known it would make you mad."

"The first day he was at school, he said we should try to be friends," Lisa said. "So he asked if he could hang with us. I told him I hated him and that he wasn't cool enough. So then he got mad and said he would join the gang just to bug me."

That explained why she had made him do the stupid test above the sewer lagoons. And why he didn't let anything she did bother him.

"Jimmy?"

"Yes?"

"The water. Pretty soon it's going to…"

"Don't say it," I said. It was almost up to my chest. She was a little taller than me, but it would be getting high on her too. "Worrying won't help."

"It's not about worrying," she said. "I wanted to tell you that maybe you should leave me."

"What!"

"This water is rising so fast, I don't think Micky will be able to get help in time," she said. "You shouldn't have to stay with me. There's no sense in both of us drowning."

The water was up to my armpits. I could not imagine how horrible it would be for Lisa. First it would reach her mouth. Then her nose.

She began to cry. "I'm scared," she said. "I don't want to die."

I couldn't leave her.

But would I let myself drown with her?

Under the water, I held her hand.

"I'm afraid too."

"I don't want to die," she said. "I don't want to die."

The water reached our necks. All I had to do was reach up for the top. I could crawl back through and save myself.

"Jimmy," she said, sobbing. "Do you think there's a God and heaven and angels and a place for me to be happy?"

I didn't know what to say. But I knew why she was asking. I learned when my dad died that it is lonely and sad and scary.

"Jimmy, don't go away." She sobbed. "Jimmy, don't leave me."

I didn't know what to do. Staying with her wouldn't help. But how could I leave? But if I didn't leave, I'd drown too.

I held Lisa close. Her tears were warm against my face.

Then a hand hit my head—a hand from above.

"Jim? Lisa? Is that you?"

It was Micky. He was coming through the opening above the cave-in.

I grabbed his hand and pulled.

Chapter Sixteen

Micky landed beside us with a splash.

I was shaking with cold. I was already on my tiptoes. The water had to be up to Lisa's neck by now.

"I got up to the street through the manhole," Micky said as he struggled to his feet. "I sent someone to get help. But I had to come back."

"We're in trouble," I told him. "I don't think we have more than a minute or two left. I can't get Lisa loose."

I explained about the concrete block that had her trapped.

"How about this," he said. "Jim, you and me both go under. With two of us, we'll get her loose."

"I don't care if you rip my foot off," Lisa said. "Do what it takes."

"All right," I said. "Micky, don't think I'm weird. But we better hold hands when we go under. Trust me, we'll be working blind."

He grabbed my hand. We both ducked under the water.

It felt like slow motion as we swirled around. Gurgling sounds filled my ears. I kept my eyes squeezed shut. I led Micky's hand to the concrete block at Lisa's feet.

We both pulled.

Nothing.

More.

Nothing.

I could not hold my breath any longer. I popped back up. But I couldn't stand without the water getting in my mouth.

I paddled.

"Jim!" Lisa cried. "The water's at my nose!"

Micky came up panting for air.

"We've got to move her!" I shouted.

"This time," Micky said. "We grab it and pull ourselves down into a squat. Plant your feet and lift, like you're trying to stand with it. Got it? Even if it breaks our backs, we don't stop lifting. And Lisa, if you feel it move, yank your foot."

We didn't give her a chance to answer.

Down into the water again.

I brought myself down to the rock. I took it in both hands. I felt Micky's hands beside me. I bumped against him as we went into the squat.

We both tried to stand. The rough edges of the concrete block tore the skin off my fingers. Still, I strained. A grunt left my mouth and bubbled air into the water.

Just a little, the concrete block shifted.

I strained harder. Micky must have done the same. Because the block shifted more.

I couldn't try it again. I needed air. I pushed up and popped above the water. Micky splashed up beside me.

"I'm free!" Lisa shouted into the darkness. "I'm free!"

Micky and I yelled and screamed with joy. If we could have seen each other, we would have been high-fiving like dancing fools.

That left one last thing. Getting out. Crawling back over this wall to the other side.

Lisa went first. Then Micky.

It was easier than on the way in. The water from Micky and Lisa's wet clothes had made the dirt slick and slippery. I wasn't scared of getting stuck.

There was only one problem. The wall was beginning to break beneath me.

I didn't know it until Lisa and Micky helped me down on the other side. I landed on the tunnel floor and splashed in a small stream of water.

In the dim light from the open manhole cover I saw water leaking through a crack in the wall. The stream was getting bigger. There was tons of water behind the wall waiting to explode onto us.

"We've got to run," I said. "If this wall goes, we're in trouble."

"My ankle," Lisa told us. "It might be broken."

Micky ducked so she could put her arm over his shoulders. I stood on the other side. She put her other arm over my shoulders.

We moved forward. She hopped at a half run between us.

I heard a rumble as we reached the ladder to the manhole.

"If the water hits," Micky shouted, "put your arms through the rungs."

Micky and I pushed Lisa onto the ladder. She began to pull herself up.

The rumble became a thunder.

Micky and I both grabbed the ladder as Lisa rose.

The thunder of the water became a roar in our ears.

"Climb! Climb!" Micky shouted.

We were a quarter of the way up the ladder when the wall of water hit, with me just under Micky.

I hooked both my arms between the iron rungs of the ladder. The water washed over me like a wall. If my arms hadn't been hooked, I would have been swept away.

The water pulled at my hair and clothes. I was still hooked in the ladder though. All I had to do was hold my breath.

Then, boom, something hit me in the legs—something with the force of a train. My last thought was short and simple. I couldn't believe the heat and pain of breaking bones.

Chapter Seventeen

"I understand you nearly died in the tunnels."

I nodded at Miss Pohl from my hospital bed. I had just woken up.

"It was close," I said.

"I understand if you'd rather not remember it out loud," she answered.

"That's all right," I said. "I'm just glad I'm here to tell you about it."

So I did. It seemed like I was talking about someone else as I described it to her.

When the rush of water had passed us by, the three of us were still hanging on the ladder. Soaked and cold but alive. Only my hooked arms kept me on the ladder, though, because I was unconscious. Later the doctors decided that a big block of concrete must have hit my legs. They guessed the water— and the block—was doing thirty miles an hour. The concrete block shattered my hip in three places.

I came back to consciousness as the medics were loading me into an ambulance. I didn't scream. I was in too much shock. I asked about Lisa and Micky, and when I was told they were okay, I decided it was all right to fall unconscious again.

"Who is Zantor?" Miss Pohl asked after I finished telling her what had happened in the tunnel.

"Zantor?" How did she know?

"I was here for a few minutes before you woke up," she said. "You were mumbling in your sleep."

"Oh." I decided not to answer.

She must have realized I didn't want to tell her, because she smiled her nice smile and changed the subject.

"You're going to miss a lot of school," she said.

"That's too bad," I said.

"You have to sound more sincere."

"Pardon me?"

"You don't sound like you're actually going to miss school. In fact, you almost sound happy about it."

Comic books all day, television when I was tired of comic books, food served to me on a tray. No tests, homework or squirming in a desk. Except for the pain in my legs, not a bad trade, especially because I could ring for a nurse whenever I wanted something.

"It's really awful that I'm going to miss school," I said, lowering my voice. A second later, I said, "Did that sound more sincere?"

"Not even close." But she was smiling.

She looked out the window, then back at me.

"Jim," she said. "You have just proved to yourself that you are a remarkable young man."

I opened my mouth, but she shushed me. "I don't think you've ever believed in yourself. But I want you to remember for the rest of your life the courage you showed, and the strength and resourcefulness you used. A lot of other people would have gone into panic. I've always known you are remarkable, and I'm glad you proved it to yourself, even though it took something terrible like this."

What does a person say to that? Fortunately, she continued talking, so all I needed to do was listen.

"It doesn't matter where a person comes from," she said. "What really matters is where a person chooses to go. Believe me, after all my years of teaching, I've seen a lot of kids grow up. Some have all the advantages—great family, money and connections—and choose to do nothing. Other kids face every and any obstacle you can imagine and choose to do what it takes to reach their dreams. And they succeed."

She smiled. "You can become whatever you want, Jim McClosky. Dream big and chase those dreams."

Again, I didn't know what to say.

"School's an important step in following those dreams," she said. "Even when you don't enjoy every minute of it, you can use what you learn in school as a foundation for all the great things you want to accomplish later in life. Understand?"

I'd never thought about these things, but it made sense, even the part about believing in myself.

"So it won't be good to miss all this class time." I knew I sounded sincere because suddenly I was.

"I think I can make you a deal," she said. "If you agree to it, I should be able to keep the social workers out of this."

"I'm listening."

And that's when she told my how I could get a passing grade by using my hospital time to put my experience into a story. She said that maybe someday I would be a writer. I asked her if she would get me a notebook and a pen, and that seemed to make her happy.

Funny enough, it made me happy too.

Chapter Eighteen

A day later, Micky walked into my hospital room with an armful of comics.

"Thought you might like these," he said. He tossed them onto my bed. "With that body cast, you're not going anywhere for a while."

"Thanks," I said. I hid my notebook. It was one thing being honest and writing things on paper. It was another to have him ask me questions about what I was doing.

"Don't thank me," he said. "Lisa and Carter got together and bought them for you."

"Lisa and Carter?"

He nodded, knowing why I sounded so surprised. "I think they're getting used to the idea of being part of a family, even though it's not a normal family."

He shrugged. "But then none of us are normal, are we?"

I thought about what some of the teachers called us: dysfunctional kids.

"No," I said, thinking the teachers might be right. "We're not."

I also thought of what Miss Pohl had said about it not mattering where a person came from, but where a person decided to go in life. "Doesn't mean we have to be that way forever, does it?"

Micky didn't answer. He pulled a chair up beside me. For a few minutes, we didn't talk.

"I've got to ask you," I finally said. "Why did you come back? Don't get me wrong. If it weren't for you, we would never have got Lisa loose. But from what you say about your dad and how you think heroes are stupid…"

I held my breath. I didn't want Micky to get mad and leave.

Micky surprised me. He grinned.

"I've been thinking about that," he said. "A lot."

He took a deep breath.

"Why did I go back? It's like this. I couldn't not do it. Does that make sense?"

I thought about why I'd kept trying to help Lisa. I nodded my head to show him I agreed.

"And I've been thinking more," he said. "About my dad."

I waited.

"All along I've been mad at him because I thought he was trying to be a hero," Micky said. "But now I don't think it was like that. It was probably the same for him as it was for us. We couldn't stand by and watch. We had to do something. Or always hate ourselves."

I nodded some more. I'd learned that bravery wasn't about the panic that might hit. It was about allowing yourself to be afraid. And not quitting because of that fear.

"You know that's what the newspapers are saying about us," Micky said. He made a face and shook his head. "But we're not heroes. It's just that other people have decided to call us that."

Micky looked at his hands and thought for a few more seconds.

"Anyway," Micky said, "for a long time I've been angry because I thought my dad died trying to be a hero. I hated him. I mean, I thought he cared so little about me and Mom that he threw his life away for the chance to be a hero."

Micky smiled sadly. "I guess I know different now, don't I?"

"Yeah," I said. "I guess so."

Micky's sad smile grew less sad. "So I don't hate him anymore. In a way, it's like having him back. Which is pretty cool after all these years."

That was all Micky said. He left me alone in the hospital room with the comics.

I picked up the top comic book. It was about a galactic soldier who never lost any battles.

I tossed the comic book onto the floor.

Micky had his father back.

Me? I didn't need Zantor anymore.